HOT WHEELS™

Dino Racing

By Ace Landers
Illustrated by Dave White

SCHOLASTIC INC.

New York   Toronto   London   Auckland
Sydney   Mexico City   New Delhi   Hong Kong

ISBN 978-0-545-25491-5

12 11 10 9 8 7 6 5   11 12 13 14/0

Printed in the U.S.A.   40
First printing, October 2010

What is the race today?

Today the cars are on the run from dinosaurs!

The cars race under a dinosaur.

Look out!
The dinosaur catches one car!

It flips the car into the air!

The other cars escape.
This is not an easy race.

Next the cars speed around a turn.

What is waiting around the next bend?

A dinosaur smashes the cars with its tail!

A racecar swerves.

The yellow car takes the lead.

Is that a bridge up ahead?

That is not a bridge!

It is a dinosaur!

The cars speed across its back.

How will the cars make it across the next gap?

The dinosaur throws the cars!

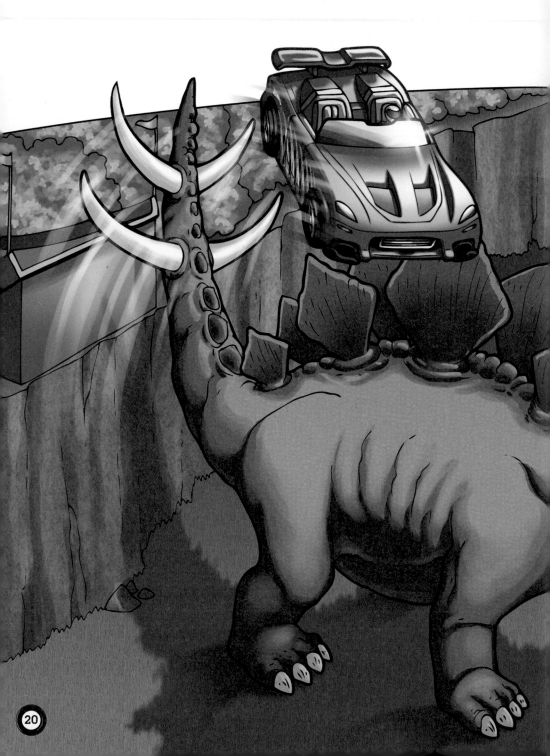

Vroom! The cars fly over the gap!

Now the course goes up above the trees.

What could be up here?

A dinosaur flies out of the clouds

The racers speed down the track.

The dinosaur grabs two cars!

It drops one car!
Where will it land?

The yellow car lands safely on the track!

Where is the blue car?

The finish line is close.

There is the blue car!

We have a winner!